HarperFestival is an imprint of HarperCollins Publishers.

Transformers: Hunt for the Decepticons: Satellite Meltdown
HASBRO and its logo, TRANSFORMERS, the logo and all related characters
are trademarks of Hasbro and are used with permission. © 2010 Hasbro.
All Rights Reserved. Printed in the United States of America.
No part of this book may be used or reproduced in any manner whatsoever without written
permission except in the case of brief quotations embodied in critical articles and reviews.
For information address HarperCollins Children's Books,
a division of HarperCollins Publishers, 10 East 53rd Street, New York, NY 10022.
www.harpercollinschildrens.com

Library of Congress catalog card number: 2010921891
ISBN 978-0-06-199179-0
Book design by John Sazaklis
10 11 12 13 14   UG   10 9 8 7 6 5 4 3 2 1
❖
First Edition

TRANS FORMERS

SATELLITE MELTDOWN

HUNT for the DECEPTICONS
TRANSFORMERS.COM

Adapted by Lucy Rosen

Illustrated by Marcelo Matere

HARPER FESTIVAL
An Imprint of HarperCollins Publishers

Deep in outer space, Soundwave grabbed a US military satellite.

With his nimble metallic tentacles connected to the dish's signal, the Decepticon robot could hear everything that was happening on planet Earth.

Soundwave listened as his master, Megatron, battled Optimus Prime for total control over the planet. Megatron was a powerful, evil warrior with tricks to defeat even the strongest Autobot—but in this battle, he was no match for Optimus Prime.

"It's time for you and your Decepticon army to leave Earth for good!" Optimus ordered.

"I don't know how we could ever repay you," he heard the Autobots' human friend Sam Witwicky tell Optimus. "The Earth owes you everything it has."

"Your friendship is greater than any gift of thanks," Optimus replied. "That is all we really need."

"Those Autobots are always working together with humans. Their friendship is what's stopping us from tearing down that silly planet!" cried Soundwave.

Soundwave said, "I bet those Autobots wouldn't be so powerful if they didn't have the trust of their precious humans." He smirked as an evil plan started to take shape in his mind.

"Destroy, Buzzsaw and Ratbat!" Soundwave commanded as he sent his minions hurtling through the Earth's atmosphere.

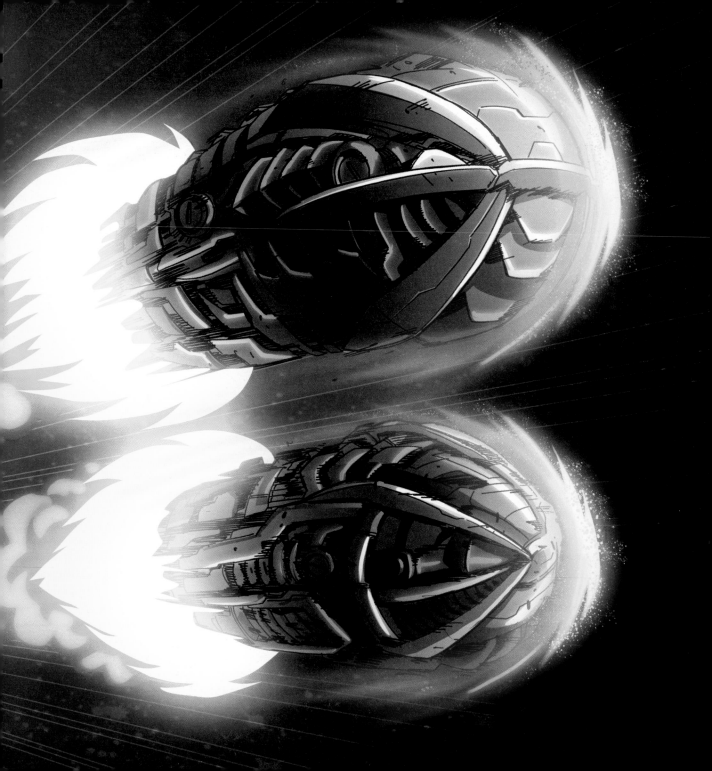

Ratbat and Buzzsaw landed in the middle of a city and began to tear down everything in their path. They smashed fire hydrants, crashed through windows, and even sent cars flying!

The police knew they had to act fast. "Call in Optimus Prime and the Autobots," they yelled into their two-way radios. "We're going to need their help!"

"Not so fast." Soundwave smirked as he listened in to the police call. Soundwave used his sharp tentacles to intercept the radio signal. He jumbled up the message the police were trying to send to the Autobots.

"Autobots, we have to roll out," Optimus said when he heard that there was trouble brewing. But instead of going to the city, where Ratbat and Buzzsaw were on a path of destruction, Soundwave sent the Autobots to an empty warehouse miles and miles away!

"Where are the Autobots?" the police cried as they desperately tried to fight off Buzzsaw and Ratbat. "Why aren't they helping us?"

Soundwave sent a new signal over all of the Earth's televisions, radios, and computers. "Your beloved Autobots have deserted you, humans!" he cried. "Surrender to the Decepticons or watch as your planet gets torn down, piece by piece!"

Sam Witwicky could not believe what he was seeing on his TV.

This can't be true, he thought to himself. *Optimus Prime would never betray his friends. Something must be wrong!*

Sam jumped into a bright yellow car with black stripes.
"Bumblebee, let's go!" he shouted.

Sam's car was no ordinary Camaro. He was really an Autobot in disguise! Together Sam and Bumblebee zoomed off to find Optimus.

Over at the warehouse, Optimus and the Autobots realized that they had been tricked. "There's no one here," Optimus said. "Someone must have sent us the wrong message—it has to be Soundwave! No other Decepticon could scramble a signal like that."

Just then, Sam and Bumblebee pulled up.
"Optimus, hurry!" yelled Sam. "Ratbat and
Buzzsaw are destroying the whole city!"

Optimus and the Autobots wasted no time. They rolled into the city just as Ratbat was throwing motorcycle after motorcycle into buildings. Without thinking twice, Optimus grabbed the Decepticon robot by his wing and flung him as far as he could go—right into Buzzsaw!

The Autobots chased away the fleeing villains.
"That takes care of that problem," said Optimus as everybody cheered. "Now to deal with the menace in outer space."

Optimus told his plan to the police. "We need the military's help. Send them a message—but not over a satellite signal!"

Soon, the military got Optimus's message. He asked them to blow up the satellite Soundwave was attached to!
"Operation Satellite Meltdown is a go," they said.
The satellite exploded before Soundwave could get any word of what Optimus had planned. "Blast those Autobots!" he cried into the darkness.

Back on Earth, Optimus and Sam smiled at each other.
"Thank you for believing in us when it looked like we had deserted you," Optimus told his friend.
"Your friendship is greater than any gift of thanks." Sam laughed. "That's all the Earth really needs!"